Collective
Amnesia

By
Al Douglas

With commentary by
Stanley J. Evans

Order this book online at www.trafford.com/
or email orders@trafford.com

Most Trafford titles are also available at major online book retailers.

Printed in Victoria, BC, Canada.

ISBN: 978-1-4251-8557-2 (sc)

*Our mission is to efficiently provide the world's finest, most comprehensive
book publishing service, enabling every author to experience success.
To find out how to publish your book, your way, and have it available
worldwide, visit us online at www.trafford.com*

Trafford Rev. 12/10/09

 www.trafford.com

North America & international
toll-free: 1 888 232 4444 (USA & Canada)
phone: 250 383 6864 ♦ fax: 812 355 4082

Dedication

Al Douglas:

To my wife, Mitos, and our son Taylor…to the sensitive souls searching for the things we know but refuse to see… who in spite of their shortcomings are willing to explore the sometimes uncomfortable truths about themselves' in search of their potential. To those who actively seek out the truth dealers who tell it like it is, even when it hurts. To those open minds unafraid to admit that they do not have all the answers. For those who don't spend too much time stuck on "what might have been!" Instead they embrace the now and anticipate the possibilities of tomorrow. It is for those who need to hear it, on behalf of those afraid to say it, and for anyone who has time to listen.

Stanley J. Evans:

To my mother, Dorothy Evans, "our" greatest cheerleader.

Acknowledgements

To my muse, "… some nights, I swear you are with me... touching me."

Thanks to all the individuals who had a hand in the creation of this body of work.

Albert Einstein, Alice Walker, Bob Marley, Maya Angelou, Ralph Waldo Emerson, Saint John The Divine, King Solomon, The Holy Scriptures…

I would like to acknowledge in particular, my wife and my best friend Stanley for always believing in my potential. Thanks for all the edits and thanks for getting feedback from potential readers. Most of all, thanks for tolerating me and my many moods.

Foreword

The New Revised Expanded edition of Webster's dictionary defines "Amnesia" as a partial or total loss of memory and defines "Collective" as a collection of individuals.

The poems and commentaries within these pages are expressions of individuals (every day people) who have suffered from a partial or total loss of memory. They have forgotten how to love and how to temper justice with mercy. They've forgotten the joy of youthful exuberance and the wisdom that comes with time.

They have forgotten time honored values or that under the skin we are one in the same. They have forgotten that there is something bigger than all of us and now they worship the creation and not the creator.

As a people, we have become self absorbed and self indulgent. These expressions will aid in reminding us about what is really important, what is really in our hearts, or what should be.

Just the thought of "Collective Amnesia" should frighten and repulse us. Through these writings, Al and I are trying to bring us back to reality and remind us that where there is life, there is hope and we must be ever hopeful.

-Stanley J. Evans
Brooklyn N.Y.

Preface

Collective Amnesia is the beginning of the literary works of a young American writer Al M. Douglas. This collection of poems presents Al to America and the world at large.

Al M. Douglas is a sensitive and insightful writer whose poems and cautionary tales will illuminate opened and closed minds. As an educator and mentor, I take a special pride in sharing these pages with my son.

Al possesses a special felicity of expression and these written works will bear this out. Throughout Al's insightful writing, I see hope for the future. Guided by the poetic goddess Maya Angelou, tempered with the emotions of James Baldwin, Imiri Baraka, and Iceberg Slim, Al manages to remain true to himself.

Al is an original, a voice "crying out in the wilderness". His style is urbane, edgy and occasionally rural. Yet, there is always a glimmer of romance and hope reflecting the cautionary cries of Curtis Mayfield, Sam Cooke, and Marvin Gaye or the moodiness of Otis Redding and the current rhythms of Jay-Z.

Even in his restless youth, Al revealed signs of social, spiritual, psychological and sexual concerns. He possesses a maturity and understanding far beyond his years. Within the confines of these pages are unguarded words. The ideas they attempt to convey are not all intended to go down entirely smooth. Themes both unfamiliar and familiar, including responsibility, actions and consequences are addressed. The object of this book is to look at everyday situations (as they affect the world, countries and ultimately the individual) from a different perspective and to gain new insights, which ultimately may lead to change.

Whether it is a change in thinking or behavior, the idea is to change for the better. Not just for the sake of changing, but for the sake of being a better human being.
Some of the reflections may awake an uneasy feeling over you. You may discover that some of the ideas call you to action. For others, you'll have to sleep on them and regurgitate them in quiet moments of contemplation. Some of the ideas presented are hard to swallow, but they need to be told.

-Stanley J. Evans

Contents

We Shared A Fish

My mother is both proud and stubborn. She never liked asking for help, she hardly complained, she bore her crosses without murmur, and when necessary, she moved with such precision to implement both blessings and beatings, you never saw her coming.

She has always been there for me and I never doubted her love, but love alone isn't enough to quiet a hungry stomach. Sometimes the hunger pains were so sharp I couldn't stand up straight, but my mother always somehow managed to keep her head high. The water to our place was shut off because of financial difficulties. The electricity was also turned off and eventually we had to move out. I wasn't sure if we were evicted as I was too young to remember but I do remember we stored our drinking water in an aquarium. Once, (unknown to us), we drank water that had mosquito larvae in it. Ironically that night, we had food to eat but I couldn't keep it down. That night I lived on the toilet.

I remember my mother ashamed and afraid the neighbors would know we had nothing. Mother would fry old onions and garlic to make the place smell good. She even pretended to go out and buy groceries. She would leave with an empty *crocus bag* and return with a bag full of crumpled paper. This gave the casual observer the illusion of a bag filled with food. But our stomachs knew better. We went to bed hungry too many nights to forget. One night to take my mind off the hunger pains, she decided we should take a walk to the wharf in downtown Kingston and try to catch a fish. Armed with some dough, a piece of string and a safety pin we went to the wharf.

The lights of downtown Kingston blurred as we hurried passed shops closed for the night. These streets were no place for an unprotected woman and a child. At nights, gunmen, with lion hair and heavy hands prowled the streets. Thieves, some with a complexion as dark as night, walked these streets. Police, with a "shoot first", "talk later" attitude walked these streets. We stayed close to the lights and once or twice, stopped to look in a store window and dream. I remember the imposing darkness of the waters near the wharf. The invisible horizon almost tricked us into thinking we could never leave. As the waves crashed against the sea wall, and splashed the salty water into the night, we had simple dreams. We dreamt of having full bellies.

We chose a spot under the light (the last place fish would hide) and we tossed our "bread upon the waters". It wasn't long before we lost the dough worm. The shiny point of the naked safety pin just wasn't enough of a lure by itself. We caught nothing. In retrospect, I don't think we ever expected to catch something but it was worth a try. We loitered long enough to dream of life beyond the horizon, and for the night to chill our bones. It was time to go home.

Just before we left, a man who was also hanging out at the wharf approached us. I don't recall the exchange of words, but I do remember him giving mom a small Styrofoam cup with a little fish as long as the bottom of the cup was round. For years I actually thought it was a gold fish. When she handed me the cup I was mesmerized by the little fish. For a brief moment, I thought of setting it free. On the way home, we discussed the fate of the fish. We reasoned that if I kept it as a pet it would die and no one would benefit, but if we ate it, then at least its death would not be in vain.

That night, we ended up eating that little fish, with no rice, no bread, and no dumplings. Mother and I ate that little fish with nothing else but love between us.

Commentary: "We shared a fish" is the first story that Al shared with me. At that time I discovered, although he has the hands of a boxer, he has the heart and soul of a poet. Also he is a gifted raconteur.

"We shared a fish" is a brief autobiographical sketch of Al tracing his relationship with his mother, his country of birth and a burgeoning career as a writer. The story describes how life shaped Al's way from the hungry little boy and a dreamer into the man whose work I believe can reshape many corners of the world! I thank God that Al M. Douglas does not suffer from "Collective Amnesia".

The Survivors

Dead babies litter the street.
Their tiny bodies strewn like garbage
Frozen in ghastly poses waiting for someone to Reach down
and pick them up.
Shell shocked women fumble through
The ruble of damaged dreams
Searching for traces of a familiar smile or frown.
It seems so unreal except that
This happens all the time.

Buried deep beneath the rubble is fear, apprehension and
hope.
Perhaps one day the sky will rain down showers of blessings
Instead of steel.
Perhaps the olive gardens will be tilled
By old men without rifles slung.
Maybe the sweet smell of figs and dates will drown the smell of
Cordite and gunpowder.
Maybe someday everything is going to be all right!

For some people searching,
All they find are dead babies.
Their tiny bodies shredded and mangled
Beyond recognition.
Here, one lies impaled.
Its hairless head and cherub face roasted.
The searching eyes have been popped
From their sockets.
Legs anchored by the weight of the debris
Ooze thick purple blood from the contorted toes.

The dead, twisted and disfigured
Litter the streets like garbage.
Potentials extinguished
Long before the fires of their imagination
Had a chance to burn.

The survivors, bandaged in blood soaked rags,
Maneuver through bomb fragments and body parts.
The smell of despair hangs heavy around their heads,
As they breathe air perfumed with dust,
Blood and scorched flesh.

Somewhere in here, beneath the mess,
Are broken dreams and promises.
Promises that could have made a difference.

Promises now lost, like the dust in the wind.

Occupied Territories

Between screaming Rocket Propelled Grenades and barking
Kalashnikovs,
Someone is crying out for more blood to be spilled.
The pain stings when lead rains down on targeted
individuals
Like women, children and innocent bystanders.
Separated behind burkhas, women grind their teeth
And squeeze blood from broken hearts.
Pain has a way of circumventing security elements
Creeping into the most secluded and secret places.

Fundamentalism tears the face off the enemy
Turning them into "rag-heads", "gooks", and "infidels".
Jihad Incorporated spreads "Death to the Zionist"
Via improvised explosive devices and sloppy beheadings…
Rebels wielding words deadlier than uranium tipped rounds
Are identified for selective targeting.

Resources are scarce.
Environmental concerns are crushed
Under the weight of Main Battle Tanks,
As the metal monsters kick up dust,
Belch smoke, and spit diesel everywhere they go.

Innocent bystanders like women, children and old men
Caught in the cross fire, are picked off one by one.
Snipers hiding in plain sight
Breathe, Relax, Aim, and Squeeze.

Both sides are pushing propaganda.
Both sides are conducting
Psychological operations or call it disinformation,
Both sides must be telling the truth.
…as long as the ratings stay high
Television networks will give you "the news as it happens."

…meanwhile,
Someone earnestly trying to find God in all of this,
Straps on a bomb and contemplates suicide as an exit strategy.

Politics

The lumbering bulldozers rumbling over
What were once our homes and schools
Kick up so much dust
It is hard to see a future anymore.

But our dreams of better days cannot get crushed
Beneath the marvel of modern machines
Even though soldiers empty magazines into
The perceived enemy
Who look like children and old men.
The walls of our dreams will not collapse…
Not under the barrage of coordinated bomb and rocket attacks,
Not under economic sanctions,
Not even under the weight of pregnant coffins.

In the streets or what is left of them,
The rivers of blood
Seem to come from everywhere,
Mixing indiscriminately
From mothers, soldiers, students, and protestors
Tinting the future a scarlet hue.

This is the result of collective punishment handed out even
To the innocent
Who are at times indistinguishable from the enemy.

Blood stains are on the hands of the guilty.
Blood stained bullet holes pepper the walls.
Blood stains color the sidewalks.
Blood stains are on a mother's hand clutching her only child.
Now gone forever.

The families of the dead want justice.
The families living want fair distribution of wealth and
services.
And sometimes, they just want blood!

The walls around our towns, though they separate families,
Cannot hide the reality that our voices are not hollow,
Our pain is not imagined and our cause may have to go
Underground.

But when we surface,
Spitting words like freedom
To erase words like checkpoint and interrogations,
Understand the truth cannot be silenced.

Although the wall has become emblematic of
Your solution to oppositional politics,
We cannot be tricked into thinking we have no rights.
We are not animals to be caged and our rage cannot be
Contained behind barricades.

The fundamentalist on all sides are attempting
To crush free speech and freedom of thought.
With the selective use of facts and
The imbalanced presentation of the issues,
Truth boils down to, "How does this affect the ratings?"
Slanted agendas are relabeled as "fair and balanced news!"

As we view our selves behind the wall we see no reflection.
We see no protection, we see no way out.
Are we to die imprisoned within ourselves?
Are we to repress our aspirations and submit to the dictates of
Those who speak peace,
But whose fundamentalist actions
Are causing revolutions to spring up like weeds?

Who is fighting for what truth anyways?

But still we dream.

Because;
Somewhere, hungry, angry, and frightened people
Want peace.
But they can't sleep because the constant raids and round-ups
Keep them up at night.
Then, they have to fight for jobs that aren't available.
Unemployment rates keep rising.
Crop yields keep falling.
Profits are grounded to dust.
Olive trees are crushed and broken
But not for peace!

Generations are choking on despair,
Caught between the stench of rotting flesh, *cordite* and
Desperation,
Many find it hard to breathe.
Clinging each day to the edge of uncertainty,
Death becomes for many a welcomed reprieve.

JANJAWID - The War In Darfur

Revelations 6: vs. 1-8 "I looked and there before me was a white horse…then came out a fiery red one. Its rider was given the power to take peace from the earth…I looked and there before me was a pale horse. Its rider was named death, and Hades was following close behind him…"

Beneath his wrinkled chocolate brow
His bloodshot eyes search the distance for what's to come
He regurgitates unfamiliar ideas and grinds rotten teeth
Praying for rest tonight.

He doesn't speak but the silence hanging heavy around his head,
Can't hide the story of loss written across his pock marked face.

Innocence is a strong and strange concept that
Resides in an unreachable corner of his memory.
The unknown is constant, sleep is scarce,
Even the desert wind is restless.

As the wind whips the sand into frenzy
You can hear ghost whispers and hooves drumming in the distant.
You can even hear the gods calling for blood to be spilled.

The wind is telling
Stories that won't make your evening news
Stories that are too serious, too graphic, too grimy… too true

The ground is shaking
The dust is stirring
The devils on horseback are coming …
You better run for your life!
The hell riders advance without ranks on horses and pickup trucks, Leaping ditches and smashing through fences.
They descend upon the defenseless
Bringing the smell of blood, sweat, and organized chaos.

The wind is telling stories that won't make your evening news.
Stories too graphic, too grimy, too true.
You won't hear
Women plead for their lives as their
Breast are chopped off.

You won't hear the screams of little girls being gang raped
Till their bodies are limp.

On the evening news you won't see
Horse and rider wheel about to the left,
Cutting down those fleeing on foot.
On the evening news you won't see
Horse and rider wheel about to the right, setting houses on fire
Shooting those who run and planting their poison in the wombs
Of Captured women.
On the evening news you won't hear the sounds of machetes
Slamming into shin bones,
You won't see the splash of blood against the blades.
You won't see the loosening of *sphincter.s*
You won't see feces running down inner thighs of someone you love…
…this isn't happening in your backyard.
You won't hear the countdown …

READY!

Children scatter to the left …

AIM!

Women run to the right…

FIRE!

The men are rounded up and executed…
The death count is higher than the definition of genocide,
But the mainstream media will never cover these stories for
Long.

Shell-shocked survivors, with blood shot eyes staring into the
Distance,
Wonder about strange words and strange ideas like "levels of
Equality, liberty and justice for all".

The devils on horseback are coming to cleanse the land and
there is no place left to hide.

Made In China

Millions are starving, girls abandoned and aborted.
Scarce resources are horded for the pleasure of few
As population control policies are enforced.

Fat bellies belonging to the elite and well connected
With appetites larger than the Three Gorges Dam
Suck the marrow from the bones of the working class.

Cheap labor and lax environmental laws draw foreign investors
Who turn a blind eye, in return for "reduced labor-costs"
And the possibilities of larger profit margins.

Consumers so far removed from these realities aren't bothered
as Long as 401-K investment plans are doing well and
Cheap goods can be purchased at Wal-Mart.

…Meanwhile, the profits from illicit arms trade are funneled
into Repressive and reeducation programs.

The government uses buzzwords to misdirect and misinform
The rest of the world,
But these empty words mean nothing to the people.

Empty words like:
"The people's republic",
"Harmonious society",
"Multilateral agreements",

But the real words are saved for the people.
Words like:
"Reeducation",
"Population control",
"Blacklist",

Words so frightening the people don't speak…

Words like:
"Propaganda"
"Censors"
"Dissident"
"Alarmist -News",
"Emergency Response Law"
"People's Liberation Army"

Dangerous words that "…endanger state security"
Are suppressed,
But sometimes the people refuse to remain docile.

With words aimed like guided missiles,
They ask for a transparent government.
They ask for an end to the abuses… they ask for their
"God given rights"…

The regime responds with force…

Engines whining, Vehicles rumble, Gears grinding,
Turrets turning, Steel creaking, Wheels crunching,
And the road moans, as it is chewed up by the weight of the
Advancing column.

Sirens flashing, boot stomping … the crowd is waiting…
Nerves are fraying.
The pungent smell of diesel and sweat mixing with

The jarring juxtaposition of sights and sounds causes
Sensory overload…

Main battle tanks and armored fighting vehicles maneuver in
the Street to corral and crush dissidents.
Armed with fire bomb ideas and words like freedom, and
Democracy,
The protestors stand their ground.

The Ministry of Public Security answers back with AK-47s
"Made in China".
These cheap tangible implements of population control in
the Hands of the People's Armed Police and The Internal
Guards
Are wielded with deadly precision.

…Blam! Blam! Blam! "Let the bodies hit the floor"
Bullets whiz by heads,
Shell casings ring as they hit the pavement,
Bullets rip into flesh, blood splatters and the world
watches…
…Blam! Blam! Blam! "Let the bodies hit the floor"

Licks from night sticks dent jawbones.
Boot heels curve back bones.
Many are rounded up and sent off to be reeducated…
Opposition will not be tolerated!

…Consumers so far removed from these realities
Watching a television "Made in China" from the safety
Of their living rooms, decorated with products "Made in
China"
Wrapped in clothing "Made in China"

Remain silent…

Tieneman Square June 5TH, 1989

"… Get up, stand up, stand up for your rights…" Bob Marley

To the "unknown rebel":

Engines thunder, windows rattle, even the earth trembles.
The tanks advance in column
Crushing the opposition beneath their tracks.

Along the route of advance the monsters spot a minor
Inconvenience in Their path
One man.
One man, unarmed and vulnerable.
One man who believed in a cause so completely
He confronted a brutal and repressive regime by planting his
feet In Defiance!
Smack dab in the path of the advancing amour column…
And for a brief moment,
This one man
Caused the world to stop and pay attention.

Female Circumcision

What dreams will drown here
In my crusted womb
A void filled with blood and pain?
What trees will grow here
In this soil spoiled with blood and tears
And will it live long enough to escape my name?

Love punctured a hole too small in my defect
And the shame hangs itself on my insides
But rancid blood and sour screams are all I have to give
As I slowly drown in a corroding pain that refuses to
subside.

The ebbing joy saps my bleeding soul
And I hold on to a hope that my tree will live,
I try to ignore the pain from my earth being plowed
But rancid blood and sour screams are what I have to give.

It has been many years since
The blunt knife repeated
Its strokes across my labia
Dropping pieces of my flesh to the ground
Already saturated in the blood of those gone before.

What trees can grow here I wonder?
What good can come from these unsacred grounds?

In the meantime
I read of women living, loving and enjoying unbridled
passion,

But I will never know such joy.

Genocide

The story of many daughters who survived the "campaigns" in places like Bosnia, Rwanda, and Zimbabwe.

He called me a whore and forced me to watch
As my mother was being torn apart with filthy objects by
Strange men.
I wanted to scream but the words stayed stuck in my throat.
They forced me to the ground and with punishing hands
Contorted my tiny adolescent body
Into strange hurtful positions.

   Passing me from one man to the next

They pumped angry flesh into all my *orifices,*
Some too small to accommodate mature pain.
Palms greased with machine gun oil muffled my cries
As they took turns
Ravishing my future.
Drowning in saliva and sweat,
Nasty lips smacked against my bony breasts,
Barely larger than plums.
There was so much pain I became numb…

   I began to forget I was alive.

When the last one pulled his penis from my mouth
I breathed blood and tasted fear.

   I wanted to die.

Then like smoke, they vanished into the night
Condemning us to live…

AIDS

Consequences are
Eating away my insides
This wasn't my choice.

…and life goes on.

Communication

"You have the right to remain silent. Anything you say can and will be used against you…"

Excerpt from the Miranda Rights

Before the age of political correctness and elusive truth
Passion boiled over into heated sentences.
Reckless conversations collided with rebel thoughts.
Cultures clashed on streets corners.
Marches happened; Batons were wrapped around skulls,
And there was productive dialogue.

Now that we have progressed to the age of litigation and
Guarded words,
We rush past the obvious.
Truth is for sale and it's all about the ratings…
Meaningful debate is replaced
With prepared questions and scripted answers.
And if a disobedient tongue spits reckless conversation,
The responsible character is skewered alive if possible.

An eye for an eye,
Rubber bullets for the protestors,
A tongue for a thought
And censorship for the dissidents…
All in the name of progress and freedom.

Truth is a contraband item that has become quite
unpopular.
Don't get caught with it,
Don't try to share it,
But then again who has time to listen.

"The world is a dangerous place. Not because of the people who are evil; but because of the people who don't do anything about it."

Albert Einstein

Woman

Against the ravishes of time and man,
You have persevered to give birth to nations.
Ideas planted in your placenta
And nurtured on love flowing from your bosom,
Find their beginnings in your arms
As you whisper divinations in a child's ear.

The universe painted it's mysteries on the walls of your
womb
And wrapped the keys of creation
Inside the umbilical cord.
The *primordial* waters were first divided inside of you after
The big bang.
Then, you pushed us out in a flood of mucus and blood.

You who wear the title of woman;
In your smile, possibilities linger.
Across cultures and time
We find you
Evolving,
Creating
And carrying the world
On your shoulders.

Know that you are loved.

Protector and preserver,
Your kisses
Stir the imagination and set blaze to emotions.
With potent stares and knowing smiles,
You add fuel to dreams and ambitions.

Goddess mothers,
Even the angels left heaven
To worship at your feet.

We your children,
Stand here as a testament
To your persistence and emotional veracity.
So rejoice,
Be exceedingly glad
For every day, the sun rises to honor you.

Behind watery eyes,
And wrinkled bellies
Even in old age, the truth remains,
You are beautiful and captivating.

With your unconditional love,
Tomorrow begins with you...who wear the title of Woman

...you are that beautiful collection of mystery,
That I can never be!

The Underground Railroad Has Surfaced

Black is the fusion of all things considered
Past, present, and future.
We pump militant fists above afros
Proclaiming our emancipation from mental slavery
In honor of the original Soul Rebels
Remember Martin, Malcolm and Medgar.

We stood in solidarity and marched a million strong
Not afraid to cry, not afraid to be responsible,
Not afraid to be men.
We embrace our future heading to the Promised Land
In honor of those who succeeded against segregation and discrimination:
Like Oprah, Maya and Condoleezza.

The Underground Railroad has surfaced.

Black is multiple shades of thought and theories
Reflecting consciousness and math, since Timbuktu,
Building pyramids, cotton gins and curling irons,
Twisting minds with intellect like dreadlocks and braids.
Black is scientific with a strong gravitational pull
Sucking you into hypnotic reggae beats, be-bop,
Twisting hip hop into mainstream.
In honor of Miles Davis, Nina Simone, and Ray Charles.

Black is devoted to truth and intimacy like Ossie Davis and Ruby Dee.
Black is beautiful and sweet,
Like mothers cooking dumplings and curry chicken
Like fathers telling stories to their children.
Black is not a myth.
And when historians pause they will say,
There lived a great people... a black people!"

Commentary: This poem was written for me to share at the High School of Enterprise, Business and Technology in Brooklyn early February 2005, in recognition of "African American History Month".

Father

To Stanley

Today is a celebration of your life, marking the occasion
when
Aeolus, father of the winds,
Whispered your potential to providence.

The Fates subsequently drew their bows and shot Cretan
arrows
Marking your moment in time.
May you find peace in your calling.

Your mystery and magic was written long before first dawn.
So we celebrate, because the years could have gone
otherwise,
And we celebrate because we realize the breath of life
Has been gifted
To you, who even angels envy.

The boy you were grew "in contrary winds",
But found strength chasing truth, and difficult dreams.

Open the Doors of memory
And remember when you were first invested with your *toga
virilis.*
Marked a man,
You became shoulders on which the future would stand.
Your love, amplified the potential of countless.
Now, much light shines because you were building "light
houses".

Transcend this life by giving shoulders to children
And let them stand upon wisdom.
Count riches by who calls you father,
See in them your elevation,
And when they fall, spread arms, which know love's labor
To catch them, even silently on occasion.

Fathers are men with roots and wings
Who create the private moments to whisper
Truth and Admonishment
To their ever emergent children
And don't sleep easy till the best, has been given.

So walk tall and unafraid,
Find your Calliope, and Clio, record your story entitled
"Misunderstood".
Cover yourself with the garlands of love sewn to
The fabrics of your memories,
Enjoy them in moments of introspection.
And live your life as it was intended.

For "It takes a long time to grow an old friend!"

Commentary: This poem was a gift from my son Al to me in celebration of my 50th birthday-9/4/56. What a great gift for one's golden jubilee. It touched my heart in such a profound manner I cannot find words to truly express my feeling, suffice it to say what a gift and expression of love and what a way to say "Happy Birthday Pop!"

"While I know myself as a creation of God, I am also obligated to realize and remember that everyone else and everything else are also God's creation."

Maya Angelou

Commentary: These next few poems should give you pause- I know it makes me nervous. We all have "Fears" and wonder what goes on "Behind Closed Doors". We've all heard about someone that suffered from "Domestic Violence", "Rape" or "Unplanned Pregnancies". We all have "Searched" ourselves internally and externally and come up short. We've been on the "Run" while running the "Rat Race". Yet, we press on towards our prize and many times we don't get it...

Fear

Although I have wings and know how to fly,
I feared the prospect of going too high.
Soaring in my thoughts but mentally bound,
I observe the other birds from the safety of the ground.

Behind The Doors

It seems so distant the times he used to love me.
Now the pain I bear inside my heart, I wished it were untrue.
The invisible blemish now imprinted on my discolored psyche Reminds me
That I,
Do not question his goings and comings.
His food must be prepared exactly right
And his every direction, even those not spoken, followed.

The slaps still sting even when he isn't striking me down.
Now he colors of my world are back and blue.
I've found my place beneath his foot
Ever since I said I do.

When I stumbled upon the realization that I was beautiful,
He lifted me with uppercuts and jabs
Till my eyes were swollen shut
And I could not find the door.

Who knows more than a woman how to care for a word like love?
He needed me so I stayed,
And every day the door got further and farther
Till I couldn't leave.

Who knows more than a man
How to reduce what was once magnificent
To something fragile and questionable
Even without saying a word?

All he has to do is look and the pain returns.

Domestic Violence

To the many victims who suffer in silence... in places they should be the most protected.

He rotated my jaw with precision guided fists.
Somewhere between the kicks and curses
That sent me sprawling across the floor
I passed out.
I awoke with tears in my lungs,
Blood in my eyes and him shoving his dick in my mouth.
So later that night
I loved him with all tricks I knew.

He became a poisonous parasite
Drawing my life away, pumping bruised blood under my
skin into My heart.
I began to die the day we met
But it felt like love at the start.

It wasn't always like this.
Somewhere after the vows,
Prison politics became his guiding light.
He was always ready to fight, even those trying to
Bandage his wounds.
His love letters were like cigarette burns in my skin
If I didn't do right by him.
But when night came
And he was screaming in his sleep,
It was in my arms he poured his pool of tears.
Now he tears my clothes looking for traces of other men.
I remember when he used to love me.
Now he beats me with angry fists that should protect
All the while telling me he loves me.

Rape

He split me open
Shredding my innocence
In search of his happiness.
Churning his issues inside me,
I tried to swallow his turgid truth,
But his angry flood choked me.
I spat out blood clots and bitter tears
Still he didn't stop.
I searched the eyes I used to love
And they came back empty.
His angry thrusting
Had blood gushing from between my thighs,
But despite my cries
I remember him climaxing
As he buried my skin into the rug.
When it was all over,
A part of my life remained trapped,
Captured in a semen stain on the floor.

Unplanned Pregnancy

He listened long enough to put his hands places
And make me feel electrified.
He tied my tongue with his turgid flesh
And told me secrets.

We spent many afternoons slapping thighs
In awkward positions,
Hoping I wouldn't get pregnant.

When I became what consequences wanted me to be,
He left me,
Just as I became ripe with seeds he planted.
Now I feel as though I'm dying faster than I'm supposed to.

As my life stands still,
I watch the world go by
Oblivious to my pain.

So on the many lonely nights, where only I
Can feel sorry for myself,
I cry for my future forever altered
And I struggle to endure.
"Surely things will change!" I keep telling myself.

As his seeds grew,
They blossomed into weeds that sucked away at my essence
Leaving just my bones and fears.
Now, lonely as the truth
I'm condemned to my years remembering
The day my life changed.

Remember When

To the many children who never gave up on themselves despite being abandoned.

In some generations the men plant no trees for their future
Instead they bury their lust inside women and cover their seeds
With empty promises.

Then they abandon the women to bear in pain alone
The fruits of the seeds planted,
When promises were warm and sweet
And kisses were meaningful.

Now and then, the seeds manage to survive and grow into children.
And sometimes there is no one to provide them shade
From the predicaments placed upon their shoulders.

But sometimes the seeds, wasted and forgotten by the wayside,
Grow majestically above the pain and misery to establish roots
And just when they begin to bear delicious fruit,
The skeptics appear with catchy phrases and their hands out
Wanting to claim a spot in the shade!

Searching

Zombies with malt liquor flowing through their veins
Thinning out the blood going to their brains
Can't walk straight or piss right.

Trying to fight the system,
They spit into the wind while cursing the invisible man
Who looks just like them.

But the mirrors in which they view themselves have been
Distorting their images for so long,
Many forgot what their beauty looks like.
So they suffocate on a glass pipe or a blunt wrapped tightly
To escape reality.
They live in the shadows of dope smoke
Choking on elusive dreams,
Selling hype and poison to our lost children,
Trying to fly with broken wings.

Terror threats and terror codes reinforce stereotypes
So we judge someone's propensity for violence based on
Their head-wrap
Or the color of their skin.
Thirty second sound-bytes,
Blink think mentality,
And heart clogging fast food,
Retards our arteries and capacity for compassion.

It is not enough to dream!

Dislocated from the truth,
The prayers of the youth are distorted into silent screams
When pedophile clergy squeeze their genitals and do
Blasphemous things.
Far too many have been forced to sit silent on the laps of those
Chosen by God.

A morality which fluctuates like mercury rising.
It should not be surprising to know the church is
Hiding from the truth
Which it never really teaches,
Because if it did,
Each of us would become our own intermediaries to God.
The Pope is just a man,
   The Imam is just a man,
      The Pastor is just a man
         The Rabbi is just a man.

And sometimes a man gets the urge to do something .....

Company profits are puffed up like lips with Botox
To look pleasing.
The collateral damage seems minor
Compared to the major gains to be made.
It doesn't seem to matter what hangs in the balance
Just as long as the shareholders are getting paid.

Wealth accumulated and acquired by greed
Gets regurgitated into the laps of those who
Conspire to commit fraud.
It's all about the bottom line,
At least that's how the investigative journalists put it
"When it's not plagiarized!"

Some would have us believe that
We must not disturb the peace!
Some would have us believe
It is not patriotic to question the elected!
And some would have us believe
We can never rise above our animal urges,
And think about something bigger than immediate
gratification.

For some, their diluted self expectations
Are reflected in wasted potential
And many are imprisoned behind a dream,
Too afraid to become the difference they wish to see,
Too afraid to see their truth
And too afraid, to ever be free…

Run -Nigga- Run

The blood was backed up in his throat.
And as the nigger hung from the rope
He choked up on shit backed up in his lungs,
Lungs that once sang songs of joy, now gargoyle
An inaudible prayer to his god
That ends before it even begins.

His life was regurgitated in the blood
That never made its way up to his throat
...the rope was too tight.

Fight the power! *(Look in the mirror)*

But his hands were tied
As ours are now tied up
In our jobs that rob us of the sacred time we find
To spend with our families.
Do you really want to see through the facade
Of this hypocrisy so called democracy?

Suspended animation: *(the state of mind in which some choose to live)*

From the tree, we see *rigor mortis*
Has forced his shit to just fallout his ass,
Pass the crack, down his legs to his feet.
Sink him deep into his own shit.
Now isn't that some shit?
Just like the shit we are in right now.
Why can't we see we are drowning in the shit?

But shit happens, just like that.
Without warning.
And it can seem charming at times
As it shines and blinds you, fools you and looks cute too…
Like BAM!!

But the shit we're in has been happening
Since way back when. All this time we ain't doing nothing,
Besides screwing around on our knees and hands,
Jerking every Tom's "dick" and Sam.
Yes Uncle Sam, he likes his coochy nice and wet

So he pimps that bitch called "society"
And the majority which includes the minorities.
Just lay back with their legs wide waiting…

A crowd looks at the body and some pelt it
With stones and insults.
Today they don't throw that many stones.
However, insults come daily disguised as laws
That causes many to feel whipped.

And as the blood clotted cow skin whip decorates and
desecrates
His black now blue,
Which one of you will rescue him?

That man is not so far removed though his flesh may have
returned to the dust.

That man is us, slowly dying, dying a terrible death.
Because we're not ready yet to do something.
And like him, we will swing from our own private trees…

…Waiting for someone to rescue us.

Rat Race

Some men I know and some I don't
Have been running their whole lives
Even before they were born

They've been running.
From warring tribes,
From slave catchers,
From apartheid,
From over-seers
From lynch mobs,
Now they run from the stickup kids.

They've been running so long
They run from shadows of themselves
Like wild animals,
Breaking Olympic records,
Breaking stereotypes,
But every day finds them behind their masks
Still running,
Running from the power of their names
Never to receive a medal for how far or how fast they ran.

Danny,
Devon,
Dwight,
All ran,
But not fast enough
To dodge the fast life standing on the corner.
They stopped long enough
To pimp their souls for the glass dick
Sucking down poison because it was easier to get high
Than to finish school.
And tomorrow they run after their first high

Which they can never catch
Still they try.

Some of these men ran
Past their history
Into the grave

Never knowing what a suit feels like,
But often dreamed of making it big.
They ran to the corner store
And bet their last dollars on numbers dreamed up in the
Salt of their tears and desperation wrinkled across their faces.

Some of these men ran so fast
Their childhood was a blur.
They grew up responsible
For so much too soon.
Now they hate the obligations they've incurred
And wait for the day
When it will all go away.
So they run over the edge and drown themselves
In the variety packs of 40 ounce malt liquor
With cool sounding names
Like Budweiser- the king of beer,
Crazy Horse, King Cobra, Olde English,
Colt 45 even introduced a 64-ounce bottle.

Danny,
Devon,
Dwight,
Ran under the steps
With hookers and porno magazines
To dream of what to do when they hit the lotto.
Cumming all over themselves and the pages
While the girls ran off to service more men and get high.

These brothers ran so fast
They never saw their own faces.
And they never stopped to see their children's faces
Decorated with bruised egos and fractured dreams.
The frightened, hungry and confused children
Thrown to the wolves of the world,
With no direction,
Begin life by Crawling, then walking,
Then running after the scared men.
And the men like the children
Were running to the arms of the unknown
Wanting to be hugged,
Wanting to be hoisted on a shoulder,

Wanting to hear "everything is gonna be all right!"

Danny,
Devon,
Dwight,
And other men, some whom I don't know
Ran from one hustle to the next
Trying to maintain a sense of normalcy
Trying to not get laid off
Trying to keep some change in their pockets
Trying not to tell somebody to "go fuck off!"
Trying to talk to God on occasions
Trying to put more than Spam on the table
Trying to get it up and keep it up
Trying to keep the baby and mother satisfied
Trying to get away from it all.

And so they ran
Away from signs that said
"No colored allowed"
"For whites only"
"Blacks enter in the rear".
They ran away from words like
"Nigger"
"Uncle Tom"
"Bastard"
"Coon"
"Lazy"
And "stupid".
They even ran away from their original names.

All these niggers running, you would have thought
The Klan wuz coming,
But the shadows wore familiar shades.
Even when they slept
They still ran
Dwight kept a gun under his pillow
He still talks in his sleep
Devon kept his shoes on in the bed
Just in case.
Never mind anybody or anything else,
Danny never slept

Because he was afraid he would die.
So he popped pills till his blood shot eyes began to bulge
from the sockets.

They all ran.
They were born running…
Spent their whole life running
And died running…
Even the father I never knew.

Before he died,
He learned to read and write.
He used to invited the divine muse to communion
And was caught up in visions
Of things to come
But he never learned to run towards the truth.

Before he died,
As he walked on the banks of the *Tallahatchie River,*
He saw Emit Till's mangled body
Hugging the murky depths
Bloated, disfigured and desecrated.
He could read well enough to understand the intent of
The repressive slave policies
Etched into the Jim Crow laws
And seared into the flesh of the young boy.

Before he died,
His vision was clear enough to see
The four girls shredded by the shrapnel in the church
bombings.

He watched helplessly
As the over-seer dressed as an officer
Sodomized Abner Louima with a plunger.
He heard them make plans
For Medgar, Malcolm and Martin
He wanted to run, but his feet were not ready
He ran to help Medgar,
But his feet were not ready,
He ran to help Malcolm,
But his feet were not ready.
And before he could reach the balcony where Martin stood,

The bullet arrived…

SLAMMING into skin and bones,
Tearing flesh as it tumbled inside,
Poisoning blood spilling the life force
And silencing for a moment
The voice of the cause.

Before I was born, my father ran.
He ran hard and fast into the arms of my mother.
And together they would run.
They ran past the bloodied martyrs,
Past the trees with their limbs,
Straining under the weight of a forbidden fruit,
Past the cotton and tobacco field,
Past the mayflower,
Past the shores of a native land,
To a time
When all men were created equal,

But after I was born,
The man I should have called father
Ran away.

Commentary:

"The footsteps of a good man are ordered by God." Proverbs

During the preparation of this book, my son and I were at loggerheads on how to proceed? What to include, what to delete and what to save?

Through reading after reading, we began to realize that there was a missing component, the representation and/or edification of the "Goodman". The everyday hero who has not been spotlighted enough. We bandied the idea about and challenged ourselves on how to proceed on this subject. We trusted our experiences, gifts and personal histories to guide us.

In my reverie, I began to think of the Barak Obama's of the world, yet the real question was, "What about the everyday man", the man (the hero) that keeps the world on its axis? The unsung heroes, those forgotten men, ignored, forgotten or unnoticed because they don't make noise, they don't make news, yet they make the world a bit brighter place for us to live in; Men such as my maternal grandfather Eddie Freeman, a good man if ever there was one.

In spite of the time or place he was ostensibly a "Freeman" in his heart, soul and mind. Given the tenor of the times (the 1920's through the 1960's) and the circumstances surrounding his living, he stood tall and was the embodiment of freedom in a time when African American people were denied basic freedoms!

In the spring of 1913 in Colombian County South Carolina, my grandfather a robust eighteen year old astride a black stallion entered my grandmother's life. She was a shy thirteen year old on the cusp of womanhood.

My great grandfather otherwise known as "Pap" the patriarch of the Powell family had promised my grandmother to a wealthy much older man (as was the custom in those days).

"Pap" gave my grandmother a clear challenge and a choice. "Would you rather be an old man's darling or a young man's slave?" She chose my grandfather opting to be a young man's slave. Yet she was never his slave. In fact she was his queen; my grandfather loved honored and cherished her from the beginning of their marriage in the autumn of 1913 until his death in the early summer of 1967. My grandfather was one of those uncelebrated "everyday heroes" who toiled as a laborer at the King saw mill in Augusta Georgia, a part time gardener and a gentleman farmer.

Along with my grandmother they raised six children, numerous grand children and times being what they were, he was always expanding the dinner table adding more chairs to welcome in and feed the hungry children in the community.

Over the years I look to my mentors, teachers, ministers and deacons, men just like my grandfather who honor their wives, love, educate and raise their children. Hard working men who did not abuse their women, who did not leave their women, or come up with a myriad of convenient unacceptable excuses for their shortcomings, orderly Masonic men who are diligent in their deportment, or that everyday man who share in the African Methodist Episcopalian experience (to name a few) throughout the United States and the Caribbean. Men we don't hear about on the evening news, even their women don't cheer them on enough. These men go unseen by many though they are not invisible yet, they are that quiet fire that will never be extinguished.

So let us take a few moments to celebrate our fathers, grandfathers, uncles, brothers and our sons, all of whom are honorable men daily, loving their wives and children, serving extended families and the nation at large with strength, courage and dignity. That quiet, every day man, that rock of Gibraltar, that king of the family who has not been presented with or taken up his crown. Men today is your coronation, take up your crown, and serve with pride.

Let us follow in your deep footsteps, those footsteps that have been ordered by God…

"The most common way people give up their power is by thinking they don't have any…"

Alice Walker

Detached

I am out of friends, though here I am
Surrounded by so many.
Who, drowning in their sorrows
Have little time for me,
Speak abbreviated words if any!

School Daze

(Valentine's Day in Manhattan Central Booking)

I learned politics on the subway,
Music, fashion, and dance at church.
I studied economics from the trigger end of a pistol,
Delved into sociology in jail
And the time I actually spent in school
I learned how to rebel.

…what I know about love hasn't quite sunk in yet.
I'm too busy surviving.

Longing

Chasing the pipe smoke to choke emotions,
For an ecstasy undeniable,
Leaving my mind numb to daily devotion.
Pipe hype never proves unreliable.

The siren's song from the bottle is sweet,
Her spirits deliver from worries fate,
Boppin heads to the psychedelic beats,
Man buys liquor, liquor makes man mate.

Most daring adventure is yet to be,
And pleasures of life too countless to list,
From scaling mountains to exploring sea,
Most pleasurable feeling I say is this…

Though the glories of the heavens hold so much,
The best feeling I've known, is a woman's touch.

After Hello

Breathtaking views arrest the imagination
As eyes volley across contours like lips.
Hues like blush quicken the pulse and boil the blood.

Hanging to the end of your stare,
The "unspoken" leans forward
And whispers what ifs and maybes…

It feels good to be alive.

Drawn to the unknown, our thoughts wander the field of possibilities
To pause or pursue.
Exposed by the lazy smile creeping across
You turn away…

Chemistry

We vibrate sympathetically like guitar strings.
Your truth resonates within the halls of my mind
And I find a comfort in your smile.
Words wrapped in beads of *Thorite*
Ignited passion and the reaction
Was more dynamic than nuclear.

Do you hear what I hear?

The truth between us turned our focus inside out.
And with each pyretic realization of
"What couldn't be",
We quietly grew swollen dreams
To have them burst open in the lonely moments,
Spilling the facts to our selves of
"What could have been?"

Ishtar

Inside the *celestial globe*
Our stars are charted light years apart
Yet our minds and hearts connected,
As if directed by the universal law of gravitation.

We were heated and hammered in the primordial fire
Linked across the space time continuum
As we moved throughout our separate lives.

We met at hello and realized
We stood on perihelion.
The light from the primordial fire
Enveloped our beings
Blinding ignorant passer-bys foolish enough to ask why?

The light seared through perineum
Exposing bundles of nerves and raw questions
That may never be answered.

Each interaction caused a progressive physiological change
In the membranes of our nerve fibers
And sensations were transmitted from receptors to
effectors…
Causing you to smile…

I smile back with a wink and a slight nod,
Knowing right then,
We had evolved.

Uncertain

Your kisses consist of sweet spirits of niter
Leaving me under a spell.
And the hunger behind your curious touch
Causes me to melt in your hands
When you plant those succulent lips on my bell.

We came this close once...
But chose not to proceed,
Now in our quiet moments we wonder to ourselves,
What if, we had done the deed?

My swollen members and beating heart will readily attest
That of all the personas that cross my gaze,
It's yours that detains my interest.

With your tendentious conversations and piquantly flavored
moods
Your presence keeps my soul aflutter,
Still, I'd prefer us not to cross that line
Which I fear could steer our *cabriolet* into the gutter.

Esther

To the high priestess, daughter of Job,
With Acacia limbs and dangerous curves,
Light my path with your eastern star.
Pour your holy oil and kisses
On my head and wherever else you please.
Meet me with courage
As we consecrate each other upon alters of flesh.
Let us sacrifice the immortality of our souls.

To have and to hold, if only for a moment.

In the year of light when we first met at the *Agora*
Near the Tower of the Winds,
The essence emanating from your smile
Left me intoxicated …
I inhaled your whispers
Then you were gone,
Only to return in my dreams as my Honored Queen.

Love Notes

The very first time
I saw possibilities
Of me, when we kissed.

Your kisses corrode
My strategic defenses
Now I'm exposed to you.

When your lips conform
To my swollen excitement
I want to explode…

Urges

(To the lady in red)

Tongues melt into lips then
Smiles upon smiles, when the thirsty lovers meet
Against the conventions of their silent soliloquies
They join in revolution, but write no eulogies.

The repented of lips locking and bodies smashing
Spill ink and sweat onto sheets
Who returns to the dust, both page and man
And the day flies bucking unless it is seized.

Skin melting into skin, writing with phallic implements
Expressions fill the lines of soft tissue page
Interlocking their rhymes love is being composed
Urania and *Erato* guiding their genius rage

Sticks turn staves then a rhyme scheme agree
When ink and paper convene
Life and death come under the pen
"The sum of our lives, but a dash in between."

Insatiable

I have a need like an itch
To get my back scratched and my cunt licked
With twisted tongues and turgid flesh!
I have a need like an itch
To feel you explode inside,
Riding my comfort to the edge of a persistent orgasm
That would last forever.
…but after all the lovers have COME and gone,
I am consumed by the lingering emptiness
And a longing to do it again.

The Artist

Inspired by an oil painting titled, "Sleeping Venus".

You painted me with your
Crooked brush
In places I thought at first
You shouldn't touch.
You stroked your brush across my lips
And I let your paint
Dribble down my neck onto my belly.
Coloring my skin with your pearls,
You smoothed out the kinks in my worries
Every time you massaged your tongue across my privates.
Now we linger on soaked sheets waiting for the paint to dry.

The Exhibitionist

Inspired by the "La Grande Odalisque" painting by J.-A.-D. Ingres.

His eyes flutter across her canvas
Sampling the sensuality oozing from her poise.
She places one of his hands on her breast,
The other between her thighs,
Guiding his attention to her pleasure principles.
He studies her and translates his understanding
Into deep slow meaningful thrusts
Giving pause to his urgency and letting it all sink in.
As she buries her nails in his back
He presses slow circles on her clitoris till her
Ground begins to shake
Sending her waves crashing against his skin.

She prostrated herself and hummed love songs into his ego
Causing time to stand still.
He held her there with his eyes tight
Mouth frozen in the middle of "aaaah…"
She exhales the night breeze as his seeds dribble
Down her succulent lips.
She kisses him and they continue to explore each other
Lost in their moment, only they exist.

Her tight thighs open even wider exposing her treasures.
Bodies collide, fault lines shifted
And the resulting tremors left the lovers
Lying breathless
Covered with a sticky nectar and gritty sand
Breathing air perfumed with sweetness only they could
create.

Unopened Love Letter #2

My fatigued fingers
Unsure of my heart's direction
Find my legs and thighs unenthusiastically sprawled

They are transformed
Into turgid fantasies
As I attempt to
Plug the emptiness
Inside my fleshy walls.

But after each release,
The peace that comes
Lingers less long
Than the one before.
I am not comforted to find you only in my dreams
When I believe you should be knocking down my door.

My heart has succumbed
To the strain of loneliness.
So each night I relive the memories
And my fatigued fingers
Unsure of their direction
Are transformed,
Into turgid fantasies.

Under My Skin

I remember once,
I turned you on
You couldn't stop coming and coming.
Like tremors in your thighs
Broke a dam and your sweet sticky love went
Flowing down your fingers;
   Slipping in and out, in and out
Of legs spread eagle.
   Your hips moved in mysterious ways
I thought you might fly away.
Now I'm running around
Looking for scraps of memories to collect
So I can fill this emptiness
Because I can't seem to get
Your smell from under my skin.

Elevator Ride

I have always wanted you
But our reality was not conducive to the situation.
So, I spent my days anxiously anticipating
The smooth melting sensation
Of your tongue roaming
My secret places.

I wish you were here.

When we finally embraced
I placed my head on your chest,
Inhaled the richness of your aroma
And listened to your heart drumming its primal song.

Even now I can still smell your vanilla, nutmeg and
cinnamon,
Lingering
With an uncompromised truth
Long after what we've done.

High Heel Boots

Whenever we kiss,
You melt on my lips like cotton candy.
Whenever we touch
You tuck your pheromones under my skin.
And whenever you purr in my ear
I tend to drift away on a sweet cool breeze.
I love it when you tease me with tickles.

I want to play you like an instrument
And plant intentions
On your intimate parts with my tongue
With our hearts beating to *spicatto* groves,
Signals turn off and on ...like "don't stop!"

With your nails embedded in my back
We make love *legato*.
Now you pull the strings to my heart
And perform *pizzicatos*.

With goose pimpled quivers, and heat
Moving down your inner thighs
I watch as ...
Blood flow builds monuments
Like erect nipples and swollen lips
Your mouth releases *staccato* moans and hisses...
As I surrender to your many flavors

Crashing Metaphors

Tonight, forget the formalities.
You and I are having a long session of "Unprotected Poetry"...

We will write our song on sheets with strange implements
Bending what is conventional we will burn desires
On the alters of flesh
To purify our souls.

Let us spill words over kisses,
Pour emotions on countertops
And stop... when our swollen members rise to the occasion
And elevate small talk ...
Till our lips crash against metaphors.

I want to run lazy circles around your nipples with my tongue
and strum your heart strings with my pick
Pushing past inhibitions and furniture.
I want to lick your cotton candy sweets, untill your juices
Linger on my face.
I will taste your sweat and salty tears as our fears connect
With windows wide and thighs exposing weakness
I'll read you like my favorite poem.

I won't care whose listening or watching.

Let's perform our play, "night and day".
Let's meet behind the horizon to swap secrets.
I will slip fingers into your gushing inkwell to write
Surprises and tell stories about smiles upon smiles

In the silence,
I want the weight of your pains to hold me.
Plant kisses and wet dreams on my skin
And I will leave more than sweetness
Sticking to your memories like
Pearls on a string.

Missing You

My beautiful man with your sunshine smile
Pressed upon my skin,
I sit here with love sprawled, deliciously aching,
Waiting for your sweet flesh to embrace.

Stung by your gentle expressions,
I miss the mystic nights I muffled my confessions in your lap
Staining fabrics with sticky emotions spilling from my lips.

My breasts are flaunting nipples, calling for your roving tongue
To search the expanse of me.
My deserts and bush are throbbing
Waiting to come alive.

My nights are spent in uneasy rest,
Dreaming of times you questioned my secret places
With your curious instrument
And urged me with just looks over the edge.
I long to inhale your residue in my bed after the morning has come.
My beautiful stallion, hurry back
I have more to give.

When the loneliness becomes intolerable,
I conjure up occasions when…
G-spot throbbing, fingers searching,
Lost in the maze of buttons and zippers,
Lips, neck, tongue tracing,
Gripping shoulders, hips rotating

Spine tingle, pulse racing,
Hands sliding, blood rushing,
Air hot, heavy breathing,
Legs shaking, clothes falling,
Fierce passion, you I'm craving.
My thighs go under water when I throw myself on your many
Moods, swollen hot and hard.

I miss your touch.
My beautiful midnight lover,
Return to me,
For the nights are becoming unbearable…

Forsaken

Like waves crashing against a defenseless shore
I am overwhelmed by emotions,
That wants more than you are willing to give.

I live with you in the bastions of my dreams
A prisoner of your truth…
Where, "what ifs" and "maybes" coerce me to
Close my eyes and imagine you still caring.
"Play…. my…. song…. I know you never go out of tune!"
I inhale the last of your fragrance still lingering on my skin,
Evoking old memories that still tantalize…

Once upon a time ago, I was intoxicated *by your kisses*
Now your lips elude me
And I am condemned to a life without you…

Soul Brother

You are the personification of goodness and man,
Wrapped in shades of chocolate skin.
Your excitement is like ice cream melted with butter scotch,
Dripping from the corners of your smile.
Each sticky drop on my lips worthwhile.
Everything about you is beautiful.
You make my toes curl up and, I don't want to wake up and
Realize , I'm stuck in someone else's dream.
You've already split my vanilla bean with your cinnamon stick
And I've tasted your eight ounces of bitter sweet chocolate.
I want more.

With your head held high, seated on Atlas shoulders
You carry fears and visions, for more than yourself.
Your inspiration sucks the air from my doubts and leaves
Only possibilities
Making me feel alive.

My raging bull, tear off my clothes and pull me through your wall,
Let me fall down on your stick till you hit the spot.
Baby, don't stop taking away my pain.
My life, my friend, my man,
What can heaven be like that you haven't already shown me?

Baby, when you and I combine,
Your chocolate milk kisses heat my soul.
My passion for you boils like pepper-infused water
Bubbling over like laughter when you touch my sides.
Place your cinnamon stick inside my love
And I'll cover your lips with my honey.
Then we'll grind skin
Till we dissolve into smiles.

I truly admire your courage my rock of Gibraltar.
Your rivers are profound.
You've challenged your dreams and reached some
And your kindness has provided light for my direction.

My man,
You are so special.
Thank you for loving and completing me.

"Relationships of all kinds-are like sand held in your hand. Held loosely, with an open hand, the sand remains where it is. The minute you close your hand and squeeze tightly to hold on, the sand trickles through your fingers. You may hold onto some of it, but most will be spilled. A relationship is like that. Held loosely, with respect and freedom for the other person, it is likely to remain intact but hold too tightly, too possessively, and the relationship slips away and is lost."

Unknown source

Life Like Ordinary People

Somewhere on the to do list
Maybe after work,
After you tell me that you are too tired
Or probably after "not right now",
I imagine,
You'll at least have a smile for me…

Even with skin on skin we've become so droning.
We lie drunk from the drained dregs of boredom's flask.
And as *Melepomene* writes our roles
For the theater of the absurd,
She dons her tragic mask and laughs.

When we couldn't keep our hands of each other,
You consumed parts of me that I still can't explain.
Now you use me till I'm raw and spent
As the reluctant assistant in a reoccurring *legerdemain.*

Chasing Shadows

I am fundamentally opposed to chasing shadows
But loving you is no different.
All I want,
Is to be there when you run
And when the morning comes,
I want to be the one
To peel away your insecurities.
I want to
Touch you in my dreams
Undress your fears and silent screams.
I want to dissect your whispers when you sleep
But…the closer I get,
The further you go.

Resolve

Across the expansive silence in *adieu,*
Between the shores of uncertainty, drift in enmity us two.
Each afraid to say to the other, truth that needs to be said.
Unable to attain a union, unleash our *adder*'s tongue instead.
Silently wishing the pain would abscond.
We pick at festering resentments, and cling to the by-gone.

With compassion in abeyance, we drift aimlessly along
Contemplating love and lost, which is truly worst?
Because some where something went terribly wrong,
Now each is waiting for the other, to abandon ship first.

Truth Is

I finally realized that after all these years
It was because of fear
I frantically clung to you.

Not because of love
Or gratitude
But because of fear.

We've become so entangled in our lies about each other
We succeeded in smothering our individual identities.
Our pain has distorted our rationales
And we choose to ignore the reality
That we are better-off separated.
So we return daily,
To this comfortable farce we both created.

Dying

It has become difficult to express my emotions
But only to you.
The Funny thing is
The closer you get, the further I do.
Inconsistent with even your lies
I try and hold on but the weight of my desperation is stronger.
So I write you this letter to tell you that I am leaving.
I find myself cowering in a dark place
Whenever you embrace me.
On the rare occasions when you do get it right,
I have to fight my desire to question your motives.
Somehow you always manage to fuck it up!
The peculiar logic of attraction has warped my senses and
Left me almost defenseless.
I really wanted us to last
Maybe this isn't our game.
I know I promised to love you
But I realize over the years you were being
Slowly consumed by my pain.

The Butcher

While under the anesthesia of your nightly injections,
The teeth on your lies separated the connective tissues
Between my logic and reason,
Tore muscles from bones and shattered my senses into a
thousand pieces.
I must admit, I have lost my mind.
Your deception slowly sliced across the grain of my heart
Till I was halved then quartered.

I watched you killing me, believing, you loved me.

You injected me with
Your mind blowing
Sense numbing
Toe tingling poison.

Still I did nothing as I realized you were eating me from the
inside literally.

You removed the fat from my flavor
Till I forgot how to smile.
Still I believed you loved me.

Numb, I watched as you crunched on the juiciest parts of
my soul
Grinding your mangled teeth into my veins
Till blood bubbled to the surface
Dark crimson droplets sliding down my wrist
Slowly draining all hope of emotional resurrection.
Now I am here all alone in a pool of my tears and rotten blood
Almost up to my neck in self pity as I try to forget how you bruised
And branded me
With what you call love.

Letting Go

When you were my one and only
With whose sweet smell my air was perfumed
I made you lord of all my thoughts
And offered my heart to be consumed.

I perfumed your sheets with lavender scents
And oiled your sun-dried skin,
But I have been blind to the lies fermenting on your lips
And fear I've already been poisoned.

(I hate you)

With what I am accused I do confess,
Indeed I love you still,
But your shifty eyes and piercing love did
The sweetest innocence kill.

Now swimming against the tides of *Acheron*
You slowly sink beneath the weight of your deeds.
For karma has stuffed your heart inside your lungs
Now you drown on consequences.

(Life's a bitch)

Pour your *agonial-respirations* into the ear of Chiron.
Tell your lies to whom you'd have believe.
No longer asphyxiated by your presence,
Your silence is a welcomed reprieve.

RIP.

Where Are You

When I was younger
And my flesh ripe and tight,
You buried your face
And throbbing anxiety between my thighs.
But now that I don't bounce like before
I spend most nights
Looking at the door
Waiting for you to come home!

Contemplating Suicide

Everything I hoped for and loved
Misery takes,
In pain I lie awake
Listening to the universe coursing through my veins
So I wonder…
Should I cut it?

But your loving has dulled my knife
And life as I once know it is not the same
Now, there is a lingering madness which stains my joy.

Once
I was tantalized by your kisses
And I saw my loneliness depart
Enchanted by your loving
I placed your world above my heart.

Once
You breathed sunshine into my smiles
And your eyes became, my moon and stars
More than air
You were my life.
Now your absence pierces like a knife
Deep into the softest part of my soul,

I can no longer hold on…

My Space

At first I resented your absence,
In truth it was a welcomed reprieve
Because I found my residuum in the silence
And at last, I can finally breathe.

Saying Goodbye

Drowning in a sea of emotions
I am confused about how our love became so unbalanced.
Somewhere between the lies and love making
I lost my direction.
You who should have been my life buoy,
Battered me with more storms than my shores could withstand.
Now, I have to let you go
Before we drown…

"...That which dominates our imaginations and our thoughts will determine our lives, and our character. Therefore, it behooves us to be careful what we worship, for what we are worshipping we are becoming."

R W Emerson

On the Level

To commit an act without a plan
When done deeds like seeds *recrudescence*
Reveals a bit about the man
Who has no thought for consequence.

Samson

Men endure grand delusions of power,
While comely eyes whisper unspoken sins,
Keep men handicapped since creations hour,
For a chance a woman might let them in.

Men leave wives they profess to love so much,
Like sheep fighting wolves they march against hell,
Mistake hell's fire for a woman's touch,
And suffer consequences much to tell.

When the soldiers bleed and nations are moved,
The might of men emerge victorious,
Good has triumphed and faith once again proved,
Die now with temptation notorious.

Time changes summer's warmth into fall's cool,
And woman since creation hath man fooled.

Casualties

Rancid thoughts bubble
In the crevices of my mind,
As I stew in my anger
Trying to recapture time lost
To an incorrigible youth.
I lost myself in her private places.
Regret erases nothing, but something
Happened that day.
Stay with me she teased!
Lips wet form wanting, waiting, and planning
Finally triumphed.
Lies never sounded sweeter coming from
A creature so beautifully maligned in design.
She tore at my heart strings exposing my soul.
I imagined I discovered the fountain of youth
As I went tumbling; eyes open
Into her dark deep hole.

Someone To Hold

I thought love was lost until I met her.
We wore the same pain cloaked in uneasy smiles
And shifty eyes.
Our conversations became the shelter for our protected hurt
As the past unraveled
Things that should never have happened.

Eventually, emotions crept
Into cavities that should have stayed rotten.
We got so close
I began to miss her.
I wanted her …breathing next to me at nights.
I wanted her… to hold me and share the silence.
I wanted her... badly before I knew why.

One day she kissed me softly
Making my pain disappear.

She feels so, so, good.
I wish I could show her off in public
Like I love her in private.
But to live here
We must remain, silent and invisible.

So I kiss my lover till next time
And return home.

Oasis

I traveled across many deserts and I'm not satisfied
With anyone else
You allow me to be free.
I only want you because
I recall long lovemaking where you unleashed me.
From my ankles,
Outlining my thighs with your tongue,
Blowing your wind across my bush,
And drinking from my spring.

Just thinking about you takes me further.

You watered my parched earth and plowed my fields
Now life springs up each time I recall.
I want you to feel my love enough to know
That you are safe in my embrace.
Whatever peace you seek may you find it here.
Thinking you in private moments
I touch myself crazy
Because you tattooed love under my skin.
My darling you,
Opened me to possibilities
Extended my boundaries
And allowed me to be free.
Thinking of you in private moments,
I want you desperately
My body thirsts for your medicine.
I have an itch,
I need that fix,
I want you.

Rosebush

You found my flowers amongst the thorniest of roses
Hiding in a maze of thistle and brush.
Lucky for me you pushed past my defenses and found
The sweetness
I hid from myself.
I knew from the first time our eyes fluttered across each
other
We were meant to be. My friend, my lover
My Cadmus butterfly,
I've died a thousand times in your arms screaming your
name
You drained my pain
Every time you injected your proboscis inside my well.
Now I've got stories to tell about what you've done to me.

In my daydreams I see you
Snaking your tongue around my charms and sensitive spots
Turning me on
Till my thighs get hot and wet.
My breasts erect nipples as you tickle my insides with your
fingers.
Even now I'm squirming as the good feelings linger.

I can still feel your lips teasing as I inhaled
Your "oohs" and "ahhs".
I exposed my truth with strange sounds when
You unraveled my mind by going down to my depths and
Snatching my breath
Kneeling between me exposed, you curl my hair and toes
Till I'm speaking words only love knows.

I find even your silence irresistible
Like the quiet words lurking behind your eyes when you
Undress me
You've got my mind pressing rewind
As I try to find all the good times,
So I can play them again.

My sweet serenade, why can't you stay with me?
I want to hold you forever, but something in you wants to
Fly away.
Naked as truth, skin on skin,
I want to pretend that it's just us,
Then reality steps in.

Consequences

Night after night
Clutching containers of "let me forget"
She leans close.
Breathing heavy,
Sweat smelling like fermented yeast,
Replaying wasted years,
She tries to have me walk in her shoes.

But there is an absence of air in the bottle.

Her thoughts decompose into slurs and frothy dribble
As she stumbles across the room to pay homage to porcelain idols,
Searching the waters as if contemplating suicide,
Clinging to its void tighter than the womb that held me.

It's so hard to breath.

I've seen her spew her insides into its porcelain maw
The same way she spits venom into my face
While reminiscing on life before me.

Why did you give me life,
When the doctor's knife could have
Saved your freedom and good looks?
It wasn't me that took your dreams away!
But in the darkness behind twisted thoughts
I pay a price
I cannot calculate, till later …

She tries to force me down
With stories and expectations
But her footsteps were never steady
And I am not ready to live with regrets.

Some night I'm sweating 50 proof
Breathing ethanol,
And erecting alters in my bathroom,
But it's too soon to have blurry vision
So I keep on searching for a way out your door.

It's so hard to breathe…

My life wants more than what you can give.

Every night she regurgitates what could have been
And reminds me of all she did not do
Because of him.
Every night she tells me,
That my smile is a constant reminder of a shameful reality
Where consequences cannot be drowned or flushed away.
She says things that ring my head even in my sleep.
Her poison digs so deep
I cry bloody tears.

When her truth serum reaches brutally intimate and honest
places
And the lumpy green vomit and frothy secretions are
Hurled at my face,
It's so hard to breathe.

When she tells it like it is,
It's so hard to breathe.

But one day,
Perhaps someday soon,
I'll find a place to call home.

Pusherman

The first time I did dope
I thought my clit was going to burst.
At first, the fire was in my brain, and then it warmed the blood
In my veins
Till I tingled
All over
And climaxed all in my hands!
Not once or twice but three times before I passed out.
This was better than his bitter chocolate melting in my mouth.
It was some kind of crazy shit
Never thought I'd take a hit before I met him.
He was an educated brother, smooth talking mother f-----!
Said he was going to change the world and some other
Sweet sounding bull sh--!
He pulled me in deeper with a few drinks and a dance.
And I jumped when the chance came for me to go home with him.

He succeeded in breaking down my drunken defenses and
I was glad he did.
It's been a long time since any one was this nice to me.
We ended up riding each other till I was weak in the knees
But he had one more trick up his sleeve.
Long, hard, shiny and cold.
I whored out my remaining will power
Since I'd let him probe me all over before.
Too late when I discovered he ejaculated fire in my veins
Leaving a *chasm* where there was only a chink before

Now I need him and he's gone.

Body Snatchers

Rue the day our souls did meet,
For destiny had already made plans
To slay the possibilities that gave life to my dreams
And snuff my budding aspirations

To the unreachable muse into whose pensive eyes I'll never stare
Between whose creamy thighs I'll never dream a little dream
Knowing I'll never feel the suppleness of your lips
I curse the fates for teasing me with what could have been

Time and distance hath restrained your tongue
But not the truth I've always known,
Our love was conceived before the Morning Star fell,
But alas, I wonder and weep alone.

Come my Prometheus; let us take back from the gods
Our fires and divine gifts held in detention
And when we rule together on the Throne of Eternity
We'll repay the gods for their cruel intentions

I long to breath deep your climactic sighs
As I rest easy upon your breasts
Falling asleep to sounds of our gentle rain
Without restrain or redress

I've never been so alive since last I died
Kiss me again and again till I burn
Why, oh why, have I been denied,
When I've never asked for what I haven't earned?

Where are you my "Love's True Love"?
Who is reaping my seeds of deeds long ago sown?
You came as close as a whisper on the wind
And just as quickly were gone.

I guess I'll see you next lifetime…

Ocean

In the great expanse of your ocean
I searched for your delitescent sweetness
To return gifts you gave before.
Tangled in the net of your choices
You dropped anchor
And almost drown.

I rowed out against your angry waves in my canoe
To pull you from the murky depths of yourself.
You reacted with foamy words that dashed me against the rocks
Broke my heart and punctured my tolerance.
Drowning in salty emotions
I tasted your gritty truth as my life slipped away
Beneath a river of tears whenever you went away.

In the great expanse of your ocean
I saw no light till I died in your flood
And was resurrected on the sandy shores of your smiles.
Loving you was mystical.

We burnt offerings to our moments on the alters of our flesh
Praying morning won't come too soon.
Murdering the pain with kisses
And initiating each other into past hurt,
We taught each other magic.

You became my madness.

…in the end,
Our waves erased the painful footprints
Stamped upon our shores.

"...A human being is a part of the whole... a part limited in time and space. He experiences himself ... as something separated from the rest, a kind of optical delusion of his consciousness. This delusion is... a prison for us, restricting us to our personal desires and to affection for a few persons nearest to us. Our task must be to free ourselves from this prison by widening our circle of compassion to embrace all living creatures and the whole of nature in its beauty."

Albert Einstein

Purpose

(To my 1ST and greatest teacher, my mother)

From all relations we build
Required duties grow
Listen to speech with a discerning ear
And consider the end before you go.

Act not against the laws of justice
Administer your obligations faithfully
For there will always be wrongs to right
And sorrow asking for sympathy.

Steel yourself today to construct tomorrow
Reap fruits of sown endeavors undeniably earned
Consider which gossamers of truth to pluck
Apply wisdom in utilizing what you've learned.

Think and learn if you can
Sow your deeds and watch them grow
Living each day to your fullest potential
To know, to know.

A Good Old Kind Of Love.

They cannot dance like they used to
But when the nights are warm arm in arm
They sit on the verandah looking out to sea
And get taken back to yesteryear when they first met

Where did all that time go?

In synchronized motions, husband and wife would
Rock back and forth
As if cares were nonexistent
Seemingly content, the lady would try to put up
Her feet to admire her shoes
These were her old and worn dancing shoes.
Now badly bruised, her feet refused to go any higher.
Try as she might they fell down any way
Was it yesterday that she was prom queen or was
The whole thing a dream?
Could this be real, was it at all real?
Gifts, the flowers, the wedding, the ring!
Oh yes the ring,
All these years, oh where was it?
Oh yes here it is,
On the, one two, third finger from her thumb
So after all she wasn't dumb.
Her king sat next to her, proud as ever,
Never left her side since the knots been tied
A love tried and proven to be the best

His head now stripped of its former glory
Is adorned by wrinkles so numerous
That his eyes have sunken to the depths of their sockets
But who can call him ugly now?
These are warrior's scars from a war fought with time

Time had already won from the beginning
But they keep defying the odds and continue making love
In smiles and in memories
Eagerly looking forward to the next together moment
Oh joy if he could get stiff again
What if she could ride again into sweet waters?
That drowned out time, place, and senses

To ride again into that unforgettable paradise place
Where they partook of ecstasy
To the place she lost her virginity to his manhood
And as long as it stood
They rode together
Past valleys, hills and mountain peaks
They go to a higher place where he could drink of her nectar
Caress her jewels with his tongue
And they would make love from night till dawn

Now, they make love in the open
Unnoticeable to anyone else but themselves

All this time
They were sitting there
Not one word was spoken
None needed be for they knew just what they had going
And they knew how far they'd come.
The old man reached over and simply touched her hand
And as the wind blew through what was left of her hair
She heard him say a thousand times ago
"I love you" and she climaxed in a tear.

Commentary: "A Good Old Kind OF Love" was the second story Al presented to me at the tender age of fifteen. A lad wise beyond his years but clearly who's heart is as old as time it self.

Allusions

What's in a word?
Laying unprepared and almost lifeless with a page for a shroud,
Dangerously dependent, upon someone
To pull the rain from its cloud.

What's in a word?
Whose possibilities are uncertain to what cause they will belong
Beneath whose surface is an undeclared intent
Until placed into a wily thought, rhyme or song.

Balancing between varied *elucidations*
The words
Perched upon the *fulcrum* of experience and expectations
    Are waiting,
        And waiting,
            And waiting…

Anonymous

Surrounded by distractions that fail to fulfill
His life is bounded by more work
Just to pay the bills.
Somewhere in the tedious routine,
He shifts into cruise control
As the world attempts to climb his shoulders,
Assuming he cares about, global poverty, fundamentalism
And the other bullshit not directly related to
His already overtaxed life.

Nipping at his heels, the demons of his reality
Have him overwhelmed and running towards an implosion.
But today, he contains his truth with loaded smiles
As the voices within ask, "When will it be your turn?"
Working his hustle and trying to maintain a sense of
control,
Validation remains always around the corner.
Maybe he'll get it right the next time.
But tonight he's running with his head buried in a bottle
Asking himself,
"Which way do I go, which way do I go?

Time

Suspended by questionable truths
We occur between life and death
Searching for what ought to be,
But the reality of our experiences
Confirms to us that nothing is absolute.

Tick tock,
  Tick tock...

To some, lives revolve like hands on a clock
Roles determined in a celestial play,
Others believe we exist unattached,
Determined by our own ways.

Tick tock,
  Tick tock,
    Time marches on...

Bound to the confines of space and time,
Our minds wrestle with the fundamental presuppositions
Who am I, what is life's purpose, and why am I here?

However, we cannot hear time as it creeps up and steals
Irreplaceable moments
Bringing us closer towards the end,
Beginning with

Tick tock,
  Tick tock.

Time does not stop to reconcile with yesterday.
Sometimes we hear the speaker
And still miss the lesson being taught
But eventually we all expire alone
Whether we go quietly or not.

Even then, time moves on between raindrops, under
Well kept secrets,
Behind the changing years
Towing us towards our inevitabilities,
Wrapped in our suspicious beliefs and curious fears.

...and the rest is silence...

Epilogue

Every poem and commentary was designed to touch upon various parts of our lives, with tears, joy, grit, gut, and grizzle. We have presented remembrances of things past and hopes for the future.

"Collective Amnesia" is a dream fulfilled. Al and I have been dreaming and planning this book for quite a while and now It has come to fruition.

It is our hope that this book will be read and discussed by many. In some ways it is a parent and child reunion and the love and joy of togetherness is overflowing. I can truly appreciate how the fathers of Tiger Woods, Michael Jordan, Reggie Jackson and Venus and Serena must feel, a father and son working in spirit and truth.
Let us awaken from our "Collective Amnesia".

-Stanley J. Evans

Glossary

Acheron:	In Greek mythology, a river in Hades.
Adder:	A type of viper.
Adieu:	The act of leaving or departing.
Agonal Respirations:	Dying breath.
Agora:	A market place and civic center in ancient Athens.
Cabriolet:	A two-wheeled, one-horse carriage with a folding top.
Cadmus Butterfly:	Type of butterfly found on the island of Jamaica.
Calliope:	In Greek mythology, the muse of epic poetry.
Celestial Globe:	Celestial globes show the positions of the stars and constellations of the night sky.
Charon:	In Greek mythology, he's the ferryman who carries the souls of the dead across the river Styx into the underworld.
Chasm:	A deep space or opening in the ground.
Clio:	In Greek mythology, the muse of history.
Cretan Arrows:	Crete; a Greek island whose inhabitants are called Cretans. The Cretans were once renowned for their archery skills.
Crocus Bag:	A burlap bag.
Cordite:	A type of slow burning powder used in ammunition as a propellant.
Delitescent:	Concealed, hidden.
Erato:	In Greek mythology, muse of love or erotic poetry.
Elucidate:	To make clear by explaining.

Fulcrum:	A pivot point.
Gossamer:	A fine film of cobweb that floats in the air.
Ishtar:	Babylonian goddess associated with love and war.
Janjawid:	Referring mostly to the conflict in Darfur. Armed militias in Sudan's western Darfur province who are accused of a series of human rights violations.
Legato:	Refers to how the instrument (such as a violin) is being played. Smooth and connected without breaks between notes.
Legerdemain:	Sleight of hand as in doing magic tricks, deceitful cleverness.
Melpomene:	In Greek mythology, the muse of tragedy.
Orifice:	An opening into a cavity in the body, like the mouth, anus, or vagina.
Perihelion:	Referring to a planet's orbital path around the Sun. It's the point where the planet in its orbit is closest to the sun. The opposite term is aphelion.
Perineum:	Very sensitive nerve rich area corresponding to the outlet of the pelvis, containing the anus and vulva or the roots of the penis.
Piquant:	An interestingly provocative flavor or lively character.
Pizzicatos:	Playing a violin by plucking rather than bowing the strings.
Primordial:	Referring to something that existed at, or from the very beginning.

Pyretic:	Pertaining to, affected by, or producing fever.
Recrudescescence:	Renewed activity like when a seed grows after being planted.
Residuum:	The remainder of something after evaporation, combustion or distillation.
Rigor Mortis:	The stiffening of the body after death.
Rue:	A feeling of regret or sorrow.
Soliloquy:	The act of speaking to oneself without addressing a listener.
Spiccato:	Playing the violin by bouncing the bow slightly from the strings.
Sphincters:	A circular type of muscle whose function is to keep close or open an orifice such as the anus.
Staccato:	Music composed of disconnected sounds.
Tallahatchie River:	A river in the United States of America that flows through the State of Mississippi. Emmet Till, a young black boy was murdered and sunk in the river.
Tendentious:	Having a definite bias for a particular thing or point of view.
Thorite:	A radioactive mineral.
Toga Virilis:	A particular toga given to Roman boys to symbolize their transition into manhood.
Turgid:	Erect, swollen, hard.
Urania:	In Greek mythology, the muse of astronomy.

About The Author

Al M. Douglas was born in Kingston, Jamaica West Indies. He migrated to the United States at the age of 10. While growing up in Brooklyn, New York, he became a father to his first child, Deborah. He has served honorably in the United States Marine Corps and Army National Guard. Al currently resides in San Diego, California.

Al is a fine and insightful writer, a visionary, dreamer and enjoys sharing his voice and God given talents with others.

About The Commentator

Stanley J. Evans has served as a Broadway Theatrical Press Agent, a member of the New York City Opera, and a producer of numerous jazz productions. Stanley takes great pride in his thirty years as an educator, mentor and administrator in the New York City Department of Education and the New York City Juvenile Justice System. Stanley is an honored member of "Who's Who in American Teachers", 2005. Working on "Collective Amnesia" with Al is a dream fulfilled.